Jarrad was kicked out of his family's home at sixteen for being gay. He struggled to survive until his adoptive family found him nearly dying in their church. They helped him get well and loved him. Jarrad studied hard and got into college. He chose nursing and planned on becoming a midwife. One afternoon after class, he got in his car and accidentally set off the car's horn. This startled a man dressed in all black who had been sleeping on the bench in front of Jarrad's car.

Jeremiah was an Amish on his Rumspringa. They became fast friends and then eventually, over time, became lovers. Their love was deep and seemed endless. Jarrad came home to celebrate the end of Rumspringa and to share the passing of his nursing boards, only to find Jeremiah was gone without a trace.

Jeremiah hadn't just left. He had written a letter. Jarrad found no letter.

After much heartache, the two moved on. They married and had families. Neither of them ever forgot the other and always wondered what had happened. Nearly twenty-eight years later, Jarrad saw paintings of himself in a quaint little Amish store—Jeremiah's store.

This book is a work of fiction. Names, characters, places, and incidents either are products of the author's imagination or are used fictitiously. Any resemblance to actual events or locales or persons, living or dead, is entirely coincidental.

Amish Love
Copyright © 2024 James Gregoryk
ISBN: 978-1-4874-4130-2
Cover art by Martine Jardin

Published by eXtasy Books Inc

Look for us online at:
www.eXtasybooks.com

Amish Love

By

James Gregoryk

DEDICATION

To my friends and family that never stopped believing in me. A special thank you to Jerry, Annika, Devin, my brother Tom and my sisters MaryPat and Kitty.

CHAPTER ONE: JARRAD'S NEW HOME

Jarrad Stewart grew up on a farm in North Dakota. One of six boys, he was number three. His parents were not overly religious but still attended mass every Sunday and holy days. They taught their sons good, solid values and how to respect themselves. They grew up working hard but still knew how to play. Jarrad felt loved.

That was, until he dropped the bombshell at fourteen that he was gay. His parents suddenly changed. They were cold and distant. Even his brothers saw the change in them. When he turned sixteen, they told him to move on with his life and that he needed to live elsewhere. There were no harsh words, no angry scenes. They basically told him that they were done with him and that he needed to go and not come back. He left with his suitcase and the three thousand dollars he'd saved. He traveled and worked odd jobs until he finally ended up in Dayton, Ohio. He lived on the streets and took shelter where he could. He didn't want to be where he was, but given his circumstances, he had little choice. Jarrad did any job that was offered to him. However, he never allowed himself to get to the point where selling his body was an option.

Seven months later, on November second, some punk kid coughed on him, and he got sick. Every day he got a little worse. The day before Thanksgiving, he knew he was very sick, but there was nothing he could do about it. He barely eked out food. He knew that he'd never afford a doctor. Jarrad was pretty sure he was suffering from pneumonia. He could hear his chest gurgle and wheeze. He knew that he was going to die. He worked his way up the street to St Mary's Catholic Church. He hoped that at least he'd get a proper burial. It took him nearly two hours to walk the couple of blocks to the church. He snuck in and lay down on one of the back pews. He collapsed into unconsciousness.

When Jarrad awoke, he heard a very soft-spoken woman gently stroking his head and telling him, "You're okay. You're going to be all right, and you're safe."

"Mama?" He looked at the woman and knew. "You're not my mom. I should've known better." He started to cry.

"I'm Sally, child. You got a name?"

"Jarrad Stewart. Dakota is what everyone calls me around here." He tried to sound tough, but it didn't seem to work.

"Again, I'm Sally, Sally Cable, and this is my husband, Fred. We found you in the church and brought you here. We need to contact someone. Do you have a family?" The woman's voice felt soothing, her smile was warm, and she had the most caring eyes.

"I do, but I'm dead to them because I'm gay." The tears just started to pour. He started sobbing and then coughing. He thought she was leaving when she stood up by his bed, but instead, she wrapped her arms around him and held him close.

"Child, if your parents kicked you out because of the fact you're gay, then there's a special place in hell for them. Do you have a number I can call?"

He hoped beyond hope that maybe they would reconsider and realize what a huge mistake they had made. He gave his parents' number to her. She dialed it right there in his hospital room so Jarrad could hear what she said. The phone rang several times, and then one of the boys answered. Sally explained what was happening and that she needed to talk to his mom or dad.

He and Sally heard, "Mom, Jarrad's in the hospital and very sick." It sounded like his little brother Reed on the phone.

He listened to his mother's voice for the first time in months. "I'm sorry we don't have a son named Jarrad, and if you bother us again, I'll call the police and file harassment charges." His mother was cold and distant.

Jarrad saw the visible anger come pouring out of Sally.

She exploded. "Fine, lady, just go ahead and call the police, but in Ohio, abandoning a sixteen-year-old is a state crime, and I *will* be filing. So, you know, bitch, North Dakota and Ohio have reciprocal agreements regarding child abuse. You'd better get an attorney." She slammed the phone down. Looking to her husband, she said, "Call Harry and sic him on that fucking bitch. I want custody of this boy by tomorrow, and I want her arrested. Somehow, someway, I want her to spend a few nights in jail at the very least."

The paperwork arrived by a special carrier two days later. Jarrad's parents had officially given him away. He wasn't their son anymore. He heard Fred tell Sally that the kids were with their grandparents, and the grandparents had pretty much disowned the parents. He also told Sally, "That bitch wailed and screamed all the way to the patrol car. She'll spend the night in the slammer."

Sally laughed until she saw Jarrad's tormented face.

"They don't want me, do they? They just threw me away like old garbage."

"I want you." Sally's words were soft and loving, and then her arms engulfed him.

His head started spinning, his chest hurt, and tears rose, "But why would you want me? I'm nothing even to my family."

"Because the good Lord led us to you, and I take that as a gift from him. So, buster, you better start acting like you're something special, as the good Lord never makes mistakes." She and Fred wrapped him in their arms. Jarrad heard Sally say to Fred. "He gave us a child."

Jarrad had to spend two more days in the hospital. Sally never left his side. The doctor finally released him, but only because Sally and Fred became his guardians. He moved out to their farm, which became his home, and he flourished.

Jarrad tried high school, but it moved way too slowly for him. So, with Aunt Sally and Uncle Fred's support, he took and passed the GED. He then passed the entrance exam to get into college. He enrolled in nursing school and did very well. Jarrad earned a full scholarship and completed his BS in record time. He was just about to turn twenty.

"We are so proud of you." Aunt Sally and Uncle Fred told him. Not a day went by that they didn't tell him how much they loved him and were so glad he came into their lives. Jarrad tried not to ever think of the people that threw him away. It was hard not to sometimes. Aunt Sally could always tell when that happened and suddenly appeared, wrapping him in her loving embrace. Jarrad loved his Aunt Sally and Uncle Fred with all his heart.

CHAPTER TWO: FINDING JEREMIAH

Jarrad walked to his car, daydreaming about the gorgeous instructor he had last semester. When he got into his car, he tossed his stuff in the back seat and then remembered his keys were in the back. He turned around to grab them, and as he did, he accidentally hit the horn, and that damn thing went off with a vengeance.

A man jumped off the bench. The guy must have been sleeping on the bench in front of his car, because he suddenly appeared and looked frightened. Jarrad let go of the horn and got out of the vehicle, scared that he might have injured the man. He hurried to see if the guy was okay. He was dressed in black and with a white cotton shirt, suspenders, black jacket, and black hat.

"I'm so sorry, reverend. I didn't mean to startle you so!" Jarrad sort of squeaked. The guy took off his hat and looked at Jarrad. The guy had the most beautiful sapphire eyes. He had dark black hair and absolutely the ugliest haircut Jarrad had ever seen. He stood tall, about 6′ 3″, and was well built as far as Jarrad could tell by his clothes. The guy glared at him at first, and then he laughed out loud. He had a big, contagious laugh. A warm and inviting laugh that made Jarrad laugh, too.

"*ACK! Ich fast meine Hose geschissen!*" he said in German.

"Amish?" Jarrad muttered to himself. "Again, I'm so sorry, but my German's very rusty."

"I speak English." He was still laughing. Maybe because Jarrad still looked a little spooked.

"I'm Jarrad Stewart, Jarrad," he said, extending his hand. The guy took it and shook his hand.

"I'm Jeremiah Berkholter."

"You're Amish, aren't you?"

"Ya, dis is true." He nodded.

"What on earth are you doing here in the parking lot? I know there's an Amish Community about fifty miles from here, but I didn't know there's one close."

"*Ach du lieben jungen englischen.* Sorry. I'm on Rumspringa and am away from the plain folk for a year to discover if I want to stay in the Amish world or not."

"Okay, so why are you here in the parking lot, sleeping on the bench?"

He looked a little scared and nervous and then blushed deep red. "Am I breaking English law? I most certainly did not mean to break any law! I'm just out of money and cannot find a job, and I need to find a place to live. I'm not a bad man. I am a gute man and did not mean to break the law. I give you my vord ov honor!"

He'd spoken all in one breath and with a German accent, but Jarrad understood what he was saying. Jeremiah's eyes were filled with tears, and his hands trembled.

"Jeremiah, you haven't broken any laws. I was just concerned that you might need some help." Jarrad realized at that moment that Jeremian was acting like the lost boy he was just four years ago, lost without friends or family to come to his aid. Fate had brought Jeremiah to him. He realized this giant working man was only about his age, lost and alone.

Jarrad realized he had stumbled into a situation. It was just so weird. One second, he was daydreaming about his nursing class instructor as he walked to his car in the parking lot of the small college he attended in Dayton, Ohio, and the next thing he knew, he was trying to figure out how he got involved with the young Amish man.

Jarrad loved most of the ideals of the Amish community, their simple way of life, and the plain clothes they wore. There were, however, a few rules he thought were stupid.

"Jeremiah Berkholter, you're coming with me."

Tears began running down Jeremiah's face.

"I've been where you are, and you need someone to come to your assistance, and I'm just the guy that can do it. I live on a farm, and they're looking for someone to help out with the chores and farm work. I can offer you a room to stay in, and from the look of you, you could use something to eat and, oh my, a bath, too."

"Nein! I cannot pay you and vill not take any handouts. Papa and Mama told me I'd sell my soul if I did!"

"Who said anything about handouts? I'm a poor college student, so anything I help you out with, you'll have to pay me back when you start working. Okay?"

He nodded.

"Let's get your stuff." He picked up a knapsack and his hat and coat. "Is that it?" Jarrad asked.

Jeremiah nodded shyly.

"Hmmm, looks like we need to head to Wally's world and get you some work clothes."

"But I do not have money for store clothes."

"Look, the people I live with took me in when I was in the situation you're in now. They helped me out, and I paid them back as soon as I could. They never asked for a dime, but I did because I have pride in who I am, like you. Only I was just sixteen and had never been away from my parents. They're like my parents now."

Jarrad's phone rang. "Hold on—Hello, Aunt Sally, what is up?"

"I need a few groceries. Flour, butter, OJ, and whole wheat bread."

"Anything else? Aunt Sal, I've found you a hired hand."

"Jarrad, are you kidding me?"

"Nope, I'm serious. He's a hardworking Amish man."

"Really? That's wonderful. Are you bringing him here to-day?" Aunt Sally sounded excited.

"Yep, be there in about an hour." Jarrad looked at Jeremiah's questioning face. "Aunt Sally was so pleased to get help. She and Uncle Fred always needed help. That's the lady that took me in. She is very pleased that you are coming to work for them!"

"So dis is your family's farm then, your Aunt and Uncle's farm?" he asked.

Jarrad saw confusion on Jeremiah's face. "Here's the long and short of me. When I was fourteen, I told my parents I was gay. When they realized I wouldn't change, they kicked me out at sixteen. I no longer have that family. They won't so much as speak to me. Sally and Fred Cable found me unconscious in their church. I'd gone there hoping God would help me or at least let me die quickly. I was very sick and had almost no money. I needed a place to live and be able to go to school. I only had enough money to pay for one meal every other day or so. Anyway, they found me and took me to the hospital, where they discovered I had pneumonia. They paid my hospital bills and took me home. They treated me like their own child. I owe them my life. They did it without conditions. I'm doing the same with you. Any questions?"

"So you sodomize men?"

Floored by his word, Jarrad furrowed his brow and said, "It's called gay."

"I know what gay is. I'm Amish, not stupid. So you're gay?"

Jarrad nodded.

"Gute, I was hoping to meet udder gay men to help me decide about myself during my Rumspringa."

Jarrad stood with his mouth gaped open.

"Vhat? You don't tink that Amish come in gay, too?" His voice had a laugh in it, and then he started that wonderful laugh of his again.

Jarrad laughed, too.

The big box store, for Jeremiah, was like taking a kid to a candy store for the first time. The first thing Jarrad did was stop at the fast-food restaurant inside. Boy, could that man eat. He wolfed down two big burgers, large fries, and a chocolate shake.

"I never ate this kind of food before. It's very gute."

Jarrad loved watching him getting into his food.

He looked at Jarrad. "Vhat? You not see a hungry man eat before?" he asked earnestly.

Jarrad laughed out loud. "I have, but I never saw anyone enjoy their food so much. I'm sorry for staring at you. I know it was rude."

"Ha, you just like looking at me," he teased.

Jarrad blushed from head to toe because it was true. He changed the subject. "Shopping time!"

Jeremiah's attention went in all directions. Jarrad kept herding him toward the men's clothing. He was scandalized when he saw men's underwear just lying out in the open. When he found bikini underwear, he thought it was a joke. "Dese vould squeeze the life out of your man parts."

Jarrad saw the twinkle in his eyes.

"Yep, We don't want that to happen, so you better go for boxers or boxer briefs. You also need jeans, shirts, socks, work boots, and a cap. Wait, you better try these on." Jeremiah slipped off his suspenders and started to lower his britches. "*Geeze*! Not here . . . in the changing room." Seeing the mischievous grin on the man's face, Jarrad realized he was teasing him. Jarrad laughed and pointed to the changing room.

Jeremiah came out looking pretty unhappy. "Dese will

pinch off my balls," he said flatly.

"So sorry, you need a much bigger size."

Jeremiah seemed to like that idea. "Ya dis iz true, much, much bigger." He laughed. The next pair fit perfectly. So they started with three pairs of jeans, four shirts, twelve undershirts, and twelve pairs of boxer briefs. He said he liked them best. He also got one pair of dress pants for church, one dress shirt, twelve pairs of socks, and a red baseball cap. He looked very pleased with it all. Jarrad paid for everything with his credit card and thought this would be a teachable moment.

When Jeremiah saw the credit card, he looked unhappy. "I do not have a card like that. Where you pay back later," he said sort of harshly.

"This is my credit card. I pay the credit card company back at the end of the month using my bank account."

"No vonder you English are always in debt. Take now, pay later is not so gute an idea."

"I'll explain all of this stuff later, okay?" Jarrad attempted to calm things down a bit.

"I told you dat I'm Amish, not stupid. I understand credit and billing accounts." He loaded the cart and started pushing it out to the car.

"Boy, what a stubborn, pigheaded, opinionated Amish man you are," Jarrad said to him.

Jeremiah stopped suddenly. Jarrad thought he would turn and explode at him. Instead, Jarrad heard him laughing,

"Ya, yust like Papa." He again broke into that laughter that made the people surrounding him laugh, too. "Yust like old Papa."

They loaded their stuff into the car and then headed to the grocery store to pick up the things Aunt Sally needed. Jarrad grabbed a cart as they entered.

Jeremiah stood there awestruck. "Gute Gott im Himmel! This is bigger than six of the biggest barns! English have to have too much to make them happy."

"Hmmm, you're a bit right, but not entirely. You see, there are foods here that the Hispanics like most, and for the Chinese, Japanese, Germans, Polish, and so on. When you live in a closed Amish-only community, you only need Amish stores."

Jeremiah blushed and said sincerely, "You are wery smart. No vonder you are in college."

It was Jared's turn to blush. They collected Sally's items and a few of their own. Jeremiah had never tasted *Kool-Aid* or root beer. Jarrad got a few of his favorite things. Jeremiah eyed him suspiciously. They got back in the car and headed for home.

"What tings will be my chores at dis farm of yours?" he asked matter-of-factly.

"Mostly milking cows and tending and feeding them, also some crop planting and hay harvesting, things like that," Jarrad answered.

"Gute, I am very gute at milking cows. I have milked cows since I was seven years old. How many do they have?"

"Mmmm, around a hundred twenty-five, give or take a few."

"Vhat? Are you crazy? No man can milk that many cows in a whole day, let alone twice a day!" Overly excited, he nearly shouted.

Teasingly, Jarrad said to him, "But I thought you were gute at milking."

He stared at Jarrad with his mouth wide open, looking at him like he had three eyes or something.

Jarrad burst into laughter. "They have equipment to milk that many cows." Jarrad thought himself quite funny and laughed and laughed.

"If we vere home, I would make you eat cow poop like I do my brudders when they get too big with their heads."

"I would punch you if you tried."

"Ack, the English are always so violent," the smug man said to him.

"And forcing someone to eat cow shit is nonviolent?" Jarrad smart-assed back at him.

"*Ja es ist*, I'm just as guilty. You'd for sure really hit me?"

"I would, and I would aim for your nuts."

"Ack, no cow shit for you then!" He laughed that rich laugh of his. "Jarrad Stewart, vill you teach me proper the English so I do not sound like such an Amish hick?" Jeremiah looked as serious as a dead man. His face said it all.

"I think your accent is rather cute," Jarrad said, but Jeremiah's expression didn't change. He looked so serious. "Yes, I can help you with that," Jarrad finally responded.

This started what would be their nearly perfect year together. They hit it off as friends immediately. Jeremiah was playful but never mean. He was funny, yet very serious when it came to work. They spent many of their free hours together. Jeremiah taught Jarrad how to pitch horseshoes and play basketball. Jarrad taught him to swim, how to cook and clean, and how to play his very favorite thing, *Monopoly*. Jeremiah hated cleaning house more than anything in the world. He did it without complaint, but the world knew he hated it. He would do anything to get out of it, but he was always playful. "Jarrad, I can't remember how to sort the laundry. Come and show me again."

Jarrad would go and sort and explain it all over again and then look up and catch his twinkling eyes. "I've been hoodwinked again."

Jarrad took Jeremiah to his very first movie. Unfortunately, it was about a Jewish family and the Holocaust. "How could the German people allow this? How were they able to stand by and allow that to happen? How will they look God in the face on the day of judgment?"

Jarrad couldn't answer those questions and told him they'd have to seek out the answers. Jeremiah talked with Sally, who went off on one of her wild, storied explanations. Uncle Fred was much better as his father fought in that war and had told him about it.

But it was Mrs. Ida Rhinefeld, a German immigrant, who really gave him the answer. "Jeremiah, I was a young girl back then. Everyone was so damned poor and tired of war debt. The Nazis gave us hope, and we took it and then realized too late that we were in a mess and we couldn't escape the situation. Speaking up would cost you your life and that of your family. So we stood silent. My Papa smuggled us out in nineteen-forty-one before the Americans joined the war. He enlisted and worked hard to rectify his mistakes, but to tell the truth, he never got over the fact that he, at one time, believed what the Nazis told everyone."

Jeremiah patted her hand and said, "I understand better now. I have some of that same guilt, never questioning because we are taught not to at a very early age, never to speak against the Amish even when you know it is wrong."

That night, something seemed to change Jeremiah. He seemed to need to be closer to Jarrad. He stood closer and sat closer. Jeremiah touched him more, not in any way out of the ordinary, just more. Several times over the next few days, Jarrad caught him staring, not that he ever looked away and just let their gazes lock. This started to make Jarrad wonder what kind of change might happen.

Jeremiah and Jarrad lived together for nearly two months. They worked together on the farm. Jarrad worked on his studies. He took an overload so he could start his nurses' rotation and then practitioners' rotation right afterward. He set goals and wanted to accomplish them as soon as he could. He told Jeremiah, "As soon as I find a full-time nurse practitioner job, I'll start studying midwifery."

"No vomen" — Jarrad's finger in the air was all it took for him to self-correct—"woman will let you stick your face down there and look around, let alone let you probe around down there," Jeremiah said so seriously.

"Yes, they will!" Jarrad snapped back. Jeremiah looked at him like he was a three-headed monster.

The next night, just an hour or so after they'd gone to bed, Jarrad heard a tapping on his door. "Jarrad, are you asleep yet?" Jeremiah whispered through the door.

"Come in. What on earth is wrong?"

Jeremiah was wearing only underwear. He had a very muscular body, and it was very hairy. Jarrad moaned at the sight.

Jeremiah stepped closer. "Are you okay?" He quietly climbed into Jarrad's bed and wrapped his arms around him. "Ah, that is so much better." Jeremiah whisper to Jarrad.

The following day, Jeremiah said, "Jarrad, I am going to be courting you from now on, just you, no von — I mean, no one else." He turned and started walking away.

"What makes you think I want to be courted by you, Jeremiah Berkholter?" Jarrad acted haughty, but he'd dreamed of this happening.

Jarrad smiled broadly when Jeremiah told him, "Because I am a gute — I mean, good man, and you already like me, and I like you, and courting is next."

"And just what am I supposed to do with the other men I am seeing?" Jarrad teased him.

It startled Jarrad when Jeremiah stormed over and stood inches away from him. "What men? No, you will not be seeing other men, just me." He thumped his chest.

Jarrad stepped even closer, and they locked gazes. "Just when did you become the boss around here?"

He engulfed Jarrad in his arms and kissed him. "No," he said, pushing Jarrad back a little. "First we court, and then we do this." He paused and looked at Jarrad from head to toe. His eyes darkened, and his nostrils flared. It was very obvious he wanted Jarrad. "Oh, to hell with that."

He picked Jarrad up, carried him to the bedroom, and placeed him on the bed. Then his huge body covered Jarrad's. Jeremiah's mouth found Jarrad's, and for the first time in his life, Jarrad understood what was meant by the word *lovemaking*. Within minutes, they were naked. Jeremiah had a perfect build, and even though Jarrad had expected it, he nearly stroked out when he realized Jeremiah was hung like a stallion.

Jarrad had no experience, and he soon realized that neither of them did. Their stiff cocks found all the right things to do to keep them going for hours.

When Jeremiah exploded with passion, it seemed to surprise him how incredible and exciting orgasms were. "Never have I felt anything more wonderful than that."

They learned about each other together.

They lay entwined with the wetness of their love between them, and Jeremiah gently spoke, "No more boyfriends, just me, right?" Jarrad nodded. "Are you ready to do this again?" His sapphire eyes expressed such passion and sincerity that all Jarrad could do was agree.

When things calmed back down, Jarrad said, "I've never really dated anyone. I've never had a romantic date with anyone and only kissed two guys before you."

Jeremiah's touch sent a sensation through Jarrad's body that no man had ever done before.

Jarrad and Jeremiah's lovemaking started out a bit clumsy and awkward at first, but both of them learned about making love to each other from each other. Jarrad realized that, unlike what he'd read in romance novels, it wasn't an instantly perfect event. They learned to love, touch, embrace, and need each other in every way possible. At first, both took the lead, but before long, Jeremiah became insatiable. He forever touched Jarrad, or he'd rub up against him, and Jarrad loved it each and every time. Jarrad soon learned that putting him off for a more appropriate time or place made that man even more passionate and aggressive when making love.

"Jeremiah, do you want to see the new movie they're showing in town?" Jarrad asked him.

"No, but I think I can show you an Oscar-winning performance in our bedroom if you let me," he said, waggling his eyebrows. Jarrad saw the deep passion in his eyes, and his gorgeous smile exuded his need. They never did get to go to the movies. Jeremiah became insatiable when it came to making love with Jarrad.

Their love grew stronger every day. Jarrad had once read that after a while, the sex part of everyone's relationship slows and becomes routine, but not his and Jeremiah's. Jeremiah continually surprised Jarrad with his ability to show love and how to make love. Sometimes, Jarrad got mad because he couldn't chase Jeremiah off with a stick. Like when he tried to study for the state boards, which he needed to pass, but Jeremiah pestered him, kissing and nuzzling him playfully.

Finally, after Jarrad put him off for a couple of hours, Jeremiah had had all he could take. "Enough, I need you." He picked Jarrad up and toted him off to the bedroom. Jarrad was so mad, but that only lasted until Jeremaih's first kiss on Jarrad's neck. His hairy warm body seemed to engulf him, and the hardness of his cock pressed against Jarrad's. They just melted into the lovemaking; the next two hours seemed to get away from them. They fit together just perfectly.

Several months into their relationship, Jeremiah suddenly realized that other people were starting to be aware that they were a couple. Being Amish, he was mortified.

"This love is only ours," Jeremiah told Jarrad. Jeremiah looked at Jarrad for agreement.

"Jeremiah, you rub up against me, and that huge piece of manhood isn't easy to hide, especially when you got that big guy all worked up. Plus, growling at men you think are just too friendly toward me is not helping keep this a secret either." Jarrad tried patiently to explain to him.

"Secret? I do not want you or us to be a secret that makes us sound dirty or sinful. It's just that Amish are quiet about our personal life. You think I am huge?" Jeremiah smirked at Jarrad.

"Huh-oh, you got that look in your eyes, and we're in the middle of the college campus. Yes, and now everyone else knows it to be true, too."

Jeremiah looked down, frowned, and turned scarlet red. "Oh, my word!" He yelped. He then took Jarrad's books from him and did the middle school book trick. Boys learned to walk with a book in front of their crotches in middle school because they had wood for about 95% of the day. "We need to get home now." He waggled those naughty eyebrows at Jarrad.

Jarrad thought that Halloween would be a hilarious time and tons of fun. He bought a mask at the store. It was a pretty realistic-looking werewolf mask. He decided to have some fun and scare Jeremiah. It was a terrible mistake on his part. He lay in wait for what seemed like hours, and just as it got dark, Jeremiah came in through the kitchen door. Jarrad hid behind the counter.

"Jarrad, you cheap little man, turn on some lights. We save no money if I break my leg in the darkness." Just as he turned on the light, Jarrad jumped up and scared him.

The blood-curdling scream Jeremiah let out was loud. *"Gott retten uns von diesem schrecklichen Übel!"* He turned and started to run for the door but suddenly stopped. "What have you done to my Jarrad?"

Jarrad heard the anger in his voice and saw it in his eyes. Jarrad was in big trouble. "Jeremiah, it's me."

Jeremiah looked angry for the first time since Jarrad met him, and even scarier was the fact that he displayed anger. "And you find this funny, how?" he snapped at Jarrad.

All Jarrad could do was squeak out, "Jeremiah, I'm sorry."

Jeremiah stood there for a few seconds, and then his anger melted away. He smirked a little and then said, "I can think of a way for you to make it up to me." Again, with the eyebrow wagging.

Jarrad listened as Jeremiah told the story to everyone that would listen about how Jarrad nearly made him shit himself with that werewolf mask. He laughed at himself. Jarrad loved the sound of his laughter. Jarrad got pranked back on Halloween night. The kids were stopping by trick or treating, and while Jarrad was busy with that, Jeremiah snuck around the house with that stupid mask, rang the doorbell, and when Jarrad answered it, Jeremiah leaped and howled. Jarrad screamed out like a nine-year-old girl. Children coming down the drive turned and fled in terror back to the main road. Jeremiah laughed until he cried. Jarrad threw that damn mask into the trash; for some reason, it wasn't funny anymore.

Jarrad loved Thanksgiving, and having Jeremiah there made it even better. Thanksgiving was so much fun. Aunt Sally, Jeremiah, and Jarrad cooked enough food to feed the army of workers and friends who came to dinner that evening. Everything was set up buffet style. People filled their plates, and just before everyone chowed down, Aunt Sally said, "We all have much to be thankful for. God bless this food and our friends and family. Amen." Each person told what they were thankful for.

Jeremiah decided that evening at the table to tell everyone they were a couple. "I don't like secrets, so Jarrad and I are a couple."

Sally burst into uncontrolled laughter, and Uncle Fred only said, "*Duh!*"

Jeremiah looked so confused.

Jarrad told him, "Jeremiah, we've talked about this. We're way too obvious to have kept that a secret."

He turned all sorts of red. But finally, everyone could hear his warm, deep laughter bubble up from inside him. "I guess we, or at least I am not as discrete as I thought we were being, huh?" Laughter filled the home. It was friendly and so inviting.

Never having celebrated Christmas like the English, Jarrad was shocked by Jeremiah's disapproval of all the decorations, trimmings, and presents, but only at first. He suddenly got into the spirit of Christmas. Jarrad came home to a house that looked like a Christmas store had exploded in it. There were decorations everywhere except on the tree. He pointed out that the tree was supposed to be decorated.

Looking puzzled, Jeremiah asked, "Why? It is so beautiful like it is with just the lights." They kept an undecorated tree.

Jarrad watched as Jeremiah got presents for everyone he could think of. He picked simple but well-thought-out gifts for everyone. They all saw the loving thought he put into each one. He got Aunt Sally a spectacular frying pan that she'd only mentioned once, and he remembered Uncle Fred had his eye on a socket set he'd wanted for years. Jeremiah's greatest surprise he saved for Jarrad. Jeremiah handed him a small, poorly wrapped present. He opened it, and inside were two gold chains, each with a half heart that fit perfectly together. When placed together, it read *Jeremiah Loves Jarrad.*

Jarrad burst into tears.

"You don't like it?" Jeremiah's voice sounded worried.

Through tears and quiet sobbing, Jarrad answered, "I have never gotten such a wonderful present in my life."

Jeremiah pulled Jarrad into his arms and kissed him right in front of everyone there. When things calmed down, Jarrad gave Jeremiah his presents. First was a framed picture of the two of them. There was so much love flowing in that picture that when he looked at it, his only word was, "Aww." Then he handed Jeremiah a small box, and his hands shook. Jeremiah took it and looked so puzzled. He opened it, and inside were two gold bands. "Are you asking me to marry you?" Jeremiah just managed to squeak out.

Jarrad nodded yes, afraid to speak.

Jeremiah took the rings, removed the gold chain from his neck, and placed them on it next to the half heart. "Jarrad, I'm in Rumspringa. I cannot answer you until it is over, not yes or no, but know this, I love you with my whole heart." That was the first time Jeremiah said the words I love you to him. Jarrad flung himself into his arms and kissed him.

"What the hell? Get a room!" Aunt Sally said, not so subtly.

"I love you, too." The room went silent, and the lights went out all but the Christmas tree. The magic of the evening flowed into carols and stories, and all could feel the love in that room.

Valentine's Day was a complete mystery to Jeremiah. He was confused about why the English had to have a day to remind them to say *I love you* to their loved ones. "This is a very stupid idea. I tell you all the time that I love you, and I do not need a special day to remind me. You English are sometimes quite stupid." However, he did spend part of that day buying Jarrad a beautiful bouquet. But of course he told everyone he planned on doing it even before he knew about Valentine's Day. His eyes lit up like a little boy when he saw the box of chocolate Jarrad got for him, and being a true Amish man, he shared with everyone who happened by over the next few days and had to tell them all about how he got it from his Valentine. Jarrad loved that man so much.

Easter arrived, and as hard as Jarrad tried to explain the Easter Bunny, Jeremiah couldn't get past how stupid that really was. "No Amish child would ever believe in such a stupid story. That rabbit would be supper," he stated matter-of-factly at the dinner table one evening.

Aunt Sally spit her water everywhere, and Jarrad thought for sure Uncle Fred was going to fall off his chair.

"Let me tell you something, Mr. Berkholter. Our kids will believe in the Easter Bunny, Santa Claus, elves, and the Tooth Fairy. You got that buster?"

"Yes, sir." He saluted me. "Wait, our kids?" The smile that went across his face said it all.

Spring had arrived, and Jeremiah had buck fever like Jarrad never experienced before. He was never without passion or the need to make love. He and Jarrad were wrapped up in each other all the time.

One morning, he said, "In two days, Rumspringa is over. Much is to be decided." He flared with passion again and made Jarrad's body sing as only he could.

CHAPTER THREE: HEARTS REALLY CAN BREAK

Jarrad arrived home very excited to tell Jeremiah about the terrific news and excited that Rumspringa was finally over. He'd finished his coursework but, even more importantly, passed his boards. He nearly didn't get the car in park before he shot out of it and dashed into the house. "Jeremiah Berkholter! I have the best news ever! Where are you?" He ran from room to room. "Stop fooling around. Damn, you must be out in the barn," he said out loud.

Returning to the living room, he saw Uncle Fred and Aunt Sally standing there. He saw they looked distraught, and Sally had tears rolling down her cheeks. "Oh God, it's Jeremiah! Has he been injured?" She shook her head no without speaking. His eyes widened with terror. "He's dead?" he squeaked out.

"No, no, my dear sweet Jarrad, he's not dead." She and Fred raced to him. "Come sit, and I will tell you what happened today. At ten this morning, an Amish buggy with two men came to the farm. Fred and I met them on the drive. One man was Matthew Berkholter, and the other was Abraham Berkholter. It turned out to be Jeremiah's father and uncle. His dad explained that his Rumspringa was now over, and they were here to collect him. When I called over to Jeremiah, he was visibly upset to see his family. They politely asked to speak with Jeremiah alone and came in here. After about two hours, Jeremiah brought me his letter of resignation and told me he was to go back with his father. He said he had no choice. I cried and hugged his neck. He whispered to me. *Tell Jarrad I will always love only him no matter where my life takes me. He is my only love forever.* I pleaded for him to wait, and when that wasn't going to happen, I begged him to tell me where he would be going. He told me he couldn't. Jarrad, that was it. He got in the buggy and left. Son, I'm so sorry." She sobbed and hugged him so hard.

Jarrad stood up, not knowing what to do. How could he go on without Jeremiah? This had to be just a nightmare that he'd awaken from. Then something hit him, and he ran to their bedroom. All of Jeremiah's English clothes were neatly folded on their bed. He hadn't noticed that before. His heart pounded so hard he couldn't hear the sounds around him. He flung open their shared closet, and the Amish clothes he had hanging there were gone, all but one hand-made Amish shirt. Pinned to the collar was a note. *For my only friend.* Jarrad found it hard to breathe. He'd known that Jeremiah might one day go back to the Amish, but he never for one second believed he wouldn't at the very least tell him about it and ask him to go with him.

That night, Jarrad found no reason to be alive in this world. The pain of living without Jeremiah overtook all reasoning. He swallowed an entire bottle of pain pills and drank a fifth of vodka.

He woke up four days later in the intensive care unit at Jefferson Memorial Hospital. He was confused and worried about Jeremiah. Jarrad knew he would be frantically worrying, but he remembered when he saw Sally and Fred walk into the room. He felt alone and dead. His Jeremiah Berkholter was forever gone from his life, and Jarrad knew that what life was before would be forever gone. Dying for him would have been a blessing.

Chapter Four: Jeremiah—Abandonment, Emptiness, Aloneness

Jeremiah's father and uncle came for him and gave him no choice but to go home with them. He'd made his sworn promise to return to Amish country to tell of his decision of either returning to the Amish community or not. Being an honorable man, he'd keep that promise. Jeremiah spent more than an hour trying to write down all he wanted to say to Jarrad in a letter. It was so difficult, and having Papa standing over his shoulder the entire time made it just that much harder. He laid the letter on the counter and gathered his belongings. Papa was always in a hurry, and he should have kept track of this hat, but he went back and retrieved it. Uncle Abraham gave him the business about getting old and forgetful.

Having to say goodbye to Sally and Fred was one of the hardest things Jeremiah had ever done. He wanted to stay and tell Jarrad what was happening, but Papa and Uncle Abraham would have none of that. They had miles to travel to get the borrowed carriage back in time to get the train back to their home.

Jeremiah hoped with all his heart that his letter would explain to Jarrad how he felt in his heart and that his Jarrad would join him soon. That night, he felt such a pain in his heart. He thought that it must be a heart attack. He felt the love he shared with Jarrad being sucked out of his soul. Just when he thought he'd better wake Papa and Uncle Abraham, it stopped, but his heart told him something had gone wrong.

His father acted so happy that Jeremiah had come home. He talked on and on about him getting baptized and joining the community. Momma was so sick he dared not argue with him to not upset her. His kind and gentle mother looked at him as if she read his thoughts. When he was a child, she saw he constantly fidgeted and never sat still. She taught him to do things with his hands, and one of those things was to do art. Jeremiah loved drawing, coloring, and painting. Papa disapproved of this frivolous activity, but Momma told him to hush, and he did. Jeremiah truly loved her so.

Fourteen days after he returned to his birthplace, his mother died very quietly without a fuss. The day after her burial, Papa started with. "It's time for you to be married and become an active member of the Amish Community." He tried to coax Jeremiah into a quick and easy decision.

He grew livid when Jeremiah told him, "I'll never be baptized, nor will I ever become an official member of the community. I'm in love with Jarrad Stewart, and there would be no other for me ever."

Every day, he walked to the mailbox, hoping for a letter from Jarrad. Every day, there was none, and his heart grew a little sadder, and the loneliness grew bigger. After nearly two months and no letter, his father said to him, "Jeremiah, you have to get your head out of the mud and realize he chose something else in life. You, my son, must do the right thing now and be baptized, marry a fine girl, and start setting into becoming an active member of the community." Papa stood with his arms folded and acted like he could make this decision for him.

Jeremiah's temper flared. "Papa, after this day, I will never speak to you of this subject again. I will not be baptized. I will live Amish in my own way. I will never marry. Do I make that clear to you!"

Papa took a step back, nodding his understanding, and walked away.

Over the next couple of years, Jeremiah's five sisters married and moved away one by one. They, like Momma, were quiet and loved being Amish. His older brothers chose different paths. The oldest, Adam, was no longer Amish and went to college and became a lawyer. Jacob married an English girl and lived on her parent's farm 50 miles from them, and Andrew went off for Rumspringa and never returned. It hurt Papa that he did not know what became of his son.

Jeremiah proved a huge disappointment to his Papa. They worked the farm and did chores but never spoke or acknowledged one another until Jeremiah made friends with an Amish girl named Lydia Vetter. They became the best of friends, and he spent hours telling her about Jarrad. She, in turn, talked about the love of her life, Anna. Anna had left the community to find work and a home for them but never returned. A couple of years later, Lydia received a letter that Anna was in love with another and would never be coming back.

Papa became overly excited about the friendship. Jeremiah told him time and time again that he and Lydia were of the same cloth and that they were just best friends. Papa would fume around the farm for days whenever he told him that. One day, Papa announced he planned to sell the farm and move away. As Jeremiah never married and he had no one to pass it on to, he would go live with his youngest daughter, Sarah.

Jeremiah felt shocked by his father's announcement, but it was his to do as he pleased. He knew that Papa believed that this threat would change his mind and make a huge turnaround in his way of thinking. That was stupid, and as his father announced it to the community, he now felt obligated to follow through, stubborn Amish jackass. The farm was sold to a young Amish couple, and Papa moved to stay with his daughter.

Jeremiah decided to move to a more progressive community. He'd saved a lot of money while working on the farm with Jarrad. He even saved more working with Papa in the past years. He found a perfect farm, not too big but just big enough, and he bought a store that sold Amish goods. At first, Lydia came to work for him and then later became his partner.

Two years into their new lives, Lydia came to him and proposed a proposition. "Jeremiah, I want to have children, lots of them, and you would be the perfect father. What do you say to that?"

He laughed. "First of all, I'm not inclined to be able to help you with that. I've made love to one person in my life, and he was my first, last, and only love."

"Jeremiah Berkholter, you do know there's more than one way to skin a deer, and I've seen some of the pictures you peek at in those not-so-well-hidden magazines you have."

Her laughter was contagious, and he couldn't help but laugh through his embarrassment. Quietly they went to the Justice of the Peace and married. They thought it best if they were going to have children.

The two proved to be a very fertile couple, and with the help of an English midwife, they conceived their first child, and the others came one after another until there were five. Jarrad, the firstborn, was named after the only love Jeremiah had ever known. Young Jarrad acted just like his mama, quiet and shy but ever so loving and very Amish. Sally Rose came next, and she acted like Papa, aggressive, bossy, and very wise for a little kid. Fredrick, their third, came out with his fists balled up, ready for a fight. He loved the farm and all the critters. Fourth came Isaac, not very Amish at all, and told his parents he planned to be a doctor, a lawyer, and a teacher.

The day their fifth child, Lydia Anne, came into the world, everything turned tragic. His best friend, the mother of his children and confidant, died bringing her into this world. It was without warning, and his family never got over it. His precious Lydia died of a massive brain hemorrhage. She died never knowing their perfect little Lydia Anne. She would have loved her so. He held his newborn daughter and wept.

Three days later, Papa arrived. Jeremiah didn't know he was coming and didn't know how he'd found out about his family's loss.

Papa turned out to be the world's greatest grandfather. Although Jeremiah could occasionally hear a tsk or two from him, he mostly didn't interfere with parenting. More importantly, he dearly loved the children. Tough, old, stubborn Papa would melt into mush when any one of his kids would say the word *Grandpapa*. He maintained his old-time Amish ways, but he didn't throw that onto Jeremiah or his children. Papa quietly moved through life, being just who he always was, perhaps a little less judgmental of others.

Time moved on quickly. Jeremiah's brood grew older. The farm made a profit, as did the store. He spent some of his time painting as he'd promised Lydia he would. She always loved the paintings he did of her and the children, and they all hung in their home. But her absolute favorites were the ones he did of Jarrad. It proved to be a very painful process as each one brought memories of Jarrad and the great love they shared. But he finished them, and he displayed them in the store.

Five years after he'd promised Lydia to keep them forever, they still brought back so many memories.

When Jeremiah pretended he did now know that Lydia

Anne's birthday would be the next day, she stomped her foot at him. "Papa, I'm going to be five tomorrow!"

"You have not lived long enough to be going on five," he told her. Jeremiah could see tears starting to well up, so he quit teasing his baby girl. It was funny how his mind could slip back in time to when he was with Jarrad, so in love, so looking forward to what he thought his life would be. Jarrad remained deep in his heart after all these years.

CHAPTER FIVE: JARRAD—LIFE WILL CONTINUE IF YOU LET IT

Because of the great love he got from Aunt Sally and Uncle Fred, he didn't die. He guessed God had other plans for him. Jarrad worked through the emptiness, loneliness, and feelings of abandonment he felt, but it took a ton of counseling and support from his wonderful parents. He still felt the pain of abandonment by his first parents and then Jeremiah, but he learned that healing takes time. He started an all-new life with the help of his wonderful adoptive parents, who were also his very best friends. Aunt Sally and Uncle Fred proved to be the best parents in the world. They encouraged him to look for his ideal job no matter where that would be.

Being a nurse practitioner and then with his midwife training, he found a great job in Carlton, near Dayton, Ohio, at a community-owned hospital where he was a full-time nurse practitioner and part-time midwife. He swore he would never look back. That, of course, was a total lie. He still missed Jeremiah every day, and sometimes, he wondered about his brothers. He rarely cried about what he lost but often wondered if they felt any loss for him.

He never called or contacted anyone or had been contacted by anyone in the bio family for many years, even though he had the same cell number the whole time. He had called once on Christmas many years ago and talked to his baby brother for about three minutes before some woman took the phone and said, "Sorry, you have the wrong number," and then hung up.

What happened to his mom, the woman who kissed boo-boos and made life better? The woman who told him every day she loved him, held him when he was scared, and rocked him when he was sick. Where was that wonderful Mama he used to know? It only hurt to look back, so he tried never to do that. And then there was Jeremiah Berkholter. He, too, had abandoned him. Jarrad nearly died when he just took off without a word. He'd never understand why he just left. He took his heart with him. Sometimes he wondered if Jeremiah ever thought about him.

Jarrad's job turned out to be the most perfect job in the world. Through his work, he found himself again. He loved everything about his job, especially the midwife part. He loved seeing new life come into this world. He really believed it made him feel alive again. The first baby he delivered would be three soon, and since that miracle, he'd seen at least adeee33 hundred more miracles. He showed pride in his work and the things he accomplished.

Aunt Sal and Uncle Fred told him nearly every day how proud they were and asked him almost every day about the job and what exciting things were happening in it, but they were worried that he was alone.

"When are you going to settle down and give us grandchildren?" He had to laugh at them, but they did mean it. At Christmas time, when he visited the farm, Uncle Fred just didn't look right. He couldn't put his finger on it, but he just seemed off. Jarrad made him promise to get a complete physical as soon as possible. He called Jarrad in April and told him he'd finally gotten a physical. "I told you, I'm just getting old. The Doc says I'm in great shape," Uncle Fred chided him.

Three years after Jarrad left the farm, his incredible father and friend, Uncle Fred Cable, died. It was sudden and quick.

He rushed home to help Sally. He knew she needed him, as Fred had been her whole life. She told Jarrad he was a big part of that, too. As he drove into the yard, he saw a huge *For Sale* sign. Sally ran out to the car and nearly yanked him out. They hugged, cried, and then talked.

"Aunt Sal, I'm moving back to help you run this farm so you don't have to sell it." Jarrad proclaimed to her like he was suddenly in charge.

"Like hell you are. Jarrad, this damn farm was Fred's dream, I loved him so much, so I followed that dream with him. But now that he's gone, I have no reason to be here. Besides, I hate the fucking cows, chickens, gardening, and any other farm shit. I'm moving to a condo, boy, and you can come with me if you want to."

Jarrad stood gaping at her, and she started laughing. He guessed deep down he always knew Sally was really not meant for farm life. In the past, they'd talked many times about her love of travel, plays, concerts, and fine dining with someone else cooking. Her current excitement and laughter filled that old house. Jarrad had to laugh, too. She made it abundantly clear that the farm would be sold.

The realtor's name was Jonathan Upton. He was the one who found the buyer who wanted the farm *as is*, and the buyer paid full price. He walked them through everything, and Jarrad found himself depending on his advice for most matters. He also discovered that he missed Jon when he wasn't around.

Sally teased Jarrad mercilessly that he just dreamed up reasons to see that fine-looking man. He guessed she was more than a little right—the farm sold in three weeks. Jarrad and Sally walked through her house, checking that everything they wanted was packed up safely. It took a lot for Jarrad to return to the little house and look around. Pretty much everything was staying. He inched his way into his old bedroom, and just as he thought he'd escape the memories of the past, Jarrad saw it. The white Amish shirt was hanging in the closet, the note still attached after all these years. *For My Only Friend,* those words still hurt so much. He was about to rip it off and throw it away when he noticed writing on the back. *I Love You, Jeremiah.*

He totally lost it. He hugged the shirt, held the note to his chest, lay on the bed with it, and cried. H wasn't sure if finding the other side of the note made him feel worse or better, but there was no time to discover that.

Jon appeared just at the right moment, just like he had since he became their realtor. His knight-in-shining-armor manner, soft smile, and gentle ways touched Jarrad's heart. He folded the shirt and tucked it under his arm. Jon walked him to his car, and he never indicated that he might have questions about that shirt. Saying goodbye was hard, but somehow, Jon made it easier as he drew Jarrad into a warm and caring embrace.

Jarrad said, "I'm going to miss the hell out of you."

Jon hugged a little tighter. "Me, too."

Jarrad arrived back in Dayton, and he already missed Sally something fierce, and Jon just about as much. He didn't have to work on Sunday and puttered around the house. The doorbell rang.

There stood Jon with a large bottle of wine and a cheese tray. "Don't just stand there gaping at me. Invite me in. Oh yeah, your Aunt Sal is on her way over, too."

"What are you doing here?" Jarrad asked.

"Ya big dope, I missed ya." About that time, Sal pushed her way in and took the wine and tray. Jarrad took that moment to wrap his arms around this wonder man's neck and kiss him.

"Could you two stop giving the neighbors a free show and

get in here?" Aunt Sal shouted from the kitchen.

Jon stuck around for a while, and when he asked Jarrad out on their first actual date, Jarrad acted like an adolescent teenager going on his very first date. Sal laughed and laughed at him.

When he came downstairs dressed and ready to go. Sal said, "You're not going to wear that outfit, are you?"

"I am."

"Where's he taking you, to the monastery?" Her smart-ass question ruffled Jarrad.

"Yes, he is," he responded.

Jon was dressed to the nines, and Jarrad could tell he had somewhere special in mind. Jarrad truly dressed very nicely, just not very showy. Jon's look showed he was very pleased with how he looked. Jarrad glanced at Sal and stuck out his tongue at her. She laughed all the way out the door.

Their first date was so wonderful and romantic that it would be forever on Jarrad's mind. Jarrad prayed that Jon didn't hear it when he accidentally called him Jeremiah; at least, he hoped not.

Jarrad and Jon officially began dating. They dated seriously, and then, about two weeks later, it hit him. Jarrad realized he was very attached and that Jon would be going home. He felt like he'd totally crumble. Sal tried to get him to beg Jon to stay or, at the very least, go with him. Jarrad couldn't do either; Jon's life was elsewhere.

One night, Jon called and told Jarrad, "I have so much to say to you."

Jarrad's heart sank. He knew this would be the end of their relationship, as long-distance relationships never work out. He cried and cried.

Jon made a grand entrance and handed him a huge

bouquet of roses, and then he made the big announcement, "I accepted a new job right here in town." Then he got down on one knee. "Jarrad Stewart, you're the love of my life. Until you came into my life, I stopped believing I would ever find someone like you. Will you marry me?"

All Jarrad could do was nod his acceptance.

Jon stayed, and they married that spring. They had made love many times before that day, but on their wedding night, it was something special. Jon took charge and took Jarrad to places he'd forgotten about. Jarrad prayed that he didn't hear him say *Jeremiah* in the throes of passion. Jarrad wouldn't hurt this incredible man for anything in the world, and Jeremiah was forever gone. Never once did he ever mention it.

Sal moved just down the road and busied her life with all the things she wanted to do, which included traveling the globe. Jon and Jarrad made a home, and they started a family. First, they got a dog named Sasha, a golden lab, and she wanted a boy to play with. She would even try to steal ones in the neighborhood, so they adopted their first child. Samson. The boy hated that name, so Jarrad suggested Samuel after his baby brother, and the boy told his new parents he loved that name, and what made it very special was that he was named after his uncle.

Samuel was a little bit of a thing when he arrived. He was about to turn five years old but looked like a toddler, but with love and patience, he prospered. It only took about a second for him to fall in love with Gramma Sally. Sally was tickled pink that she had a grandbaby to spoil. She smiled and hugged him.

She became even more overjoyed when five-year-old Fanny Bea came to them six months after they got Samuel. She was a spitfire just like Sally, and the two butted heads all the time, but when Sal started calling her Anna Marie, that tiny girl fell in love with that name. They bonded so closely that Jarrad felt a little left out. Anna Marie, it was. Sal had chosen both Jarrad's and Jon's grandmother's names.

Sometimes he would sit back and laugh until he cried listening to the two of them. "Girl, you're the most belligerent child. Do you know that?" Gramma Sal would say to her.

"I'm not begent you are!" little Anna Marie would snap back.

Samuel was their quiet and thoughtful child. He liked rules and followed them to the letter. He also let anyone know when they were not in compliance. He and Anna Marie fought like tom cats but adored each other at the same time, even though Samuel tried to drown Anna Marie in the kiddy pool more than once. Anna Marie, in turn, beaned him in the head with a rock, a bat, a baseball, and a crescent wrench. He had to get stitches several of those times. They had a special love-hate relationship. God help anyone that hurt or crossed their sibling.

By age seven, they had separate lives and friends, so nearly all the bickering had ceased. Samuel was into baseball, gymnastics, and science. His time with friends was very valuable to him, and he guarded it from everyone in the household. Anna Marie, on the other hand, was a *fly-by-night* type of person with her friends. She loved drama, numbers, and was a killer basketball player. Her best friend changed nearly daily. She came into her own when she discovered the stage. Oh my, what an actress she turned out to be. With two very diverse children, the number of games, plays, competitions, fairs, and field trips were too many to count anymore. Jon, Jarrad, and Gramma Sal attended and loved every one of them.

One trip proved to be very hard for Jarrad. Samuel's class took a trip to an Amish village. Seeing the Amish people brought back memories of Jeremiah. It sparked the sad memories of lost love and loneliness he thought had long ago disappeared. Jon, ever near, was there to put him back together and just loved him. Jarrad loved that man so much.

Through the years, Jon was always there, his loving, caring, sweet man who filled his heart with joy and his body with passion. Samuel was about nine the first time he told them, "Get a room!" They laughed until they cried.

The kids grew up, and his precious Sally grew old. One day, fifteen years after the sale of the farm, the head of the hospital division called Jarrad to the ER *STAT*. Jon and the kids had found Sal lying on the floor of her condo after she'd had a massive stroke. Jarrad saw by the expression in Sally's eyes that she wanted nothing done, but he couldn't just let her go.

She lay in the ICU for six days. She regained some of her power of speech. Though very slurred, they could understand her. "My boy, Jarrad, you know I love you with all my heart, right?" He nodded through tears. "Good, cuz I'm going to go be with Fred now. Take care of Jon and my grandbabies." She closed her eyes and was gone.

Once again, Jarrad felt that terrible feeling of being abandoned, but there was Jon engulfing him, loving him, and letting him need him. They had the funeral back home, and she was buried next to her beloved Fred. Jarrad felt so left behind once again. His ever-faithful Jon helped him pick himself up and continue.

Five days later, they returned home. Jarrad watched the door as he still expected Sal to barge through it anytime. It never happened, and sadness filled Jarrad's heart. The night that Jarrad received the package from Sal's attorney, he fell apart. Sal left him everything she had, and it was all worth millions. It meant that the two of them, Sal and Fred, had saved and scrimped just for him. He'd rather have had them here longer. Sal's only request in her will was that both kids go to the best schools possible, and in his heart, he promised her they would.

Through the years, their kids teased Jarrad about how he dressed. "God, Dad, what are you? Amish or what?" Samuel said one night as they went out to eat.

His sister was not much better. "Dad, are you joining the priesthood with that hideous outfit?" Her hands went up and down to make her point about what she thought of the entire outfit.

Jarrad liked simple and plain. That was who he was. Jon, on the other hand, loved stylish and colorful clothes. "You always make me stand out like a peacock," he would tease. But Jarrad liked himself and who he was, so he'd never changed.

The fall that Samuel and Anna Marie turned fifteen, Jarrad's baby brother arrived on their doorstep. The doorbell rang, and Anna Marie answered it.

"Dad! Come here! Quick!"

Jarrad panicked and ran quickly to his daughter, as did Jon and Samuel. They all looked terrified. But there he stood, Jarrad's baby brother, Sammy. The brothers looked so much alike that it scared the family. They kept looking back and forth from Sammy and then back to Jarrad. The brothers stood there staring at each other, and then the same sound came from both. It sounded almost wild animal-like, but it was a sound of joy, and they flung themselves into each other's arms. They just held on and cried, not wanting to be the first to let go.

Sammy was a grown man, handsome and tall. "Jarrad, I'm so glad to see you. I missed you something terrible," Sammy murmured into Jarrad's neck.

"What took you so long to come to me?" Jarrad blubbered.

"Mom and Dad wouldn't bend about us seeing you. They would have divided the family even more and made our lives more miserable. Some of us younger ones lived with Gramma and Grandpa Stewart until they passed away, and then we had to go back to the folks. But now that they're dead, nothing is stopping us. The rest will be here tomorrow. I'm the test case to see if you still want to see us."

Jarrad made a sound filled with pain as he sobbed. First, for the loss of his parents, may God not judge them too harshly, and then for the fact his family wanted to see him. Jon took him from Sammy and engulfed him. Jarrad needed him, and Jon knew it. When Jarrad finally controlled his emotions, he introduced his family to their uncle and brother-in-law. "Sammy, this is my family. This is Jon, my husband and the best man I know." Jon shook his hand and welcomed him to the family. "This is our daughter Anna Marie. She's named after Gramma Stewart and Jon's Grammy Marie Upton." He hugged her, and being the pistol-Pete she was, she hugged him right back. "And this is Samuel, named after you."

Jarrad saw the tears quickly well up in Sammy's eyes.

"Y-y-y-you named your son after me?" He managed to squeak out before pulling Samuel in close and hugged him, and then tears started up again.

"Uncle Sammy, you're smothering me." Samuel matter-of-factly stated.

The two brothers talked for hours about the family and how they all were. It was such a feeling of completeness.

The next morning, at eight sharp, Jarrad and Jon heard horns honking outside their house. They stepped out with Sammy and saw Jarrad's four other brothers standing there together, looking so much like Jarrad it was almost like looking in the mirror. Jarrad stood there frozen on the porch, bawling like a three-year-old, unable to move, and they seemed frozen, too. Jarrad pointed to them, looked at Jon, and then pointed to them again.

"Honey, you need to go to them," Jon said as he gently

pushed him in their direction. It then seemed he had wings and flew to them, first hugging the oldest Mitch, then Reed, then Darrin, and last Pauly. The sounds of joy and past hurt escaped from them and filled the yard. Suddenly, Jarrad's children and husband were there, and the yard filled with nephews, nieces, sisters-in-law, and brothers-in-law. There were hugs and more tears and laughter and more hugs and more tears. It was one of the best days of Jarrad's life. He had his family back. They all walked to the house. Jarrad quietly prayed. "See, Mom and Dad, I'm a good person and wonderful to know. Too bad you two will never get to know that." While embracing his husband, Jon heard Jarrad and said, "Amen."

They spent the next few years getting to know each other; brothers have a special bond, and Jarrad discovered it couldn't be broken.

Chapter Six: Life Goes On

As the kids grew up, they were great students throughout high school and eventually went to college. Samuel left first; he was off to premed school. Their beautiful daughter, Anna Marie, went off to study accounting, of all things. Jon's business was now huge, and Jarrad was eternally busy at the hospital delivering babies. Jarrad guessed they worked so much because it was lonely without the kids. The kids had always been a major part of their lives, and now the nest was empty, awaiting for the someday grandkids. Although they loved their time alone together. The years flew by so quickly that Jarrad hardly noticed.

Jarrad had just finished delivering Jacob Kyle Whinestein. He was a home birth and went off without a hitch. As he got into his car, his phone rang. It was Samuel, so he answered it. "Hello, my son. What can I do for you?" He chirped at him.

"Pop, it's Dad. He's on his way to the hospital. Pop, it doesn't look so good. You need to hurry."

Somehow Jarrad went into his professional mode. "Son, I'll be there in less than seven minutes. Where's your sister?"

"Papa, she's on her way, too. I called all the rest of the family, too. Hurry." Now came the reality of the seriousness of the situation. Jarrad got a terrible tightness in his throat. If his son, the doctor, was worried, then it was bad. He started to reach panic mode. Jarrad stepped on it and actually got there before everyone else.

Beth Johnson, head of the ER, met him at the door. "Jarrad,

41

it's bad, honey. He's had a massive heart attack, and he re-
fused any treatment, and he's asking for you."

"Take me to Jon." That was all he could manage to say.
There was the man he loved, ashen gray and struggling to
breathe.

"I waited for you, Jarrad."

"Jon, you have to let them treat you," Jarrad begged.

"Please, Jarrad, let me say all of this while there's still
time." He struggled so hard. Jarrad tried to stop him, but he
gave Jarrad his *shut up and listen* look.

"Jarrad, you've always been the real love of my life. I loved
you from the minute I first saw you. I know you love me
deeply, but I wasn't the first love you had in your life, and I
hope now you'll go and find him and tell him that you still
care about him, Amish or not." He pulled Jarrad down and
kissed him and then simply stopped living. At first, Jarrad
was confused by his total silence, but then he heard their children's cries of anguish, and he knew that the person who'd
loved him totally unconditionally had gone to be with God,
and his heart broke. Jarrad laid his head on Jon's chest and
cried.

The funeral was not a funeral at all but a celebration of
Jon's life. Their children had arranged it all. Jarrad found it
hard to cope those first few days after his husband left him
alone in this world. Medication and family support got him
to that celebration, and as he watched it unfold into the beautiful presentation they'd developed, it gave him some inner
peace. Everyone who knew him had something wonderful to
say.

When Jarrad's turn came, he talked to Jon. "You promised
never to leave me alone. I guess this was one promise that you
couldn't keep. I love you, Jon. Say Hello to Sal and Fred. Jon,
watch over our kids and keep them safe."

His beautiful children joined him as they followed Jon's casket to the hearse and then to the gravesite. He was okay until they lowered his casket into the ground. "God, please wake me from this nightmare I'm living!" With his son on one side and his daughter on the other, they led him to the car. He sat silently during the ride home, and then there they were on each side again, getting him into the house. Jarrad kissed both of them and went upstairs to the bedroom.

Halfway up the stairs, Anna Marie asked him, "Papa, are you okay?"

"No, baby girl, I'm not, but I will be, with you two here." He went to the room, his and Jon's bedroom, and gently closed the door behind him. He knew his children worried about him and were a little confused, but so was he. He needed to see if he could feel Jon in their room. He started touching the things that belonged to Jon. He smelled his clothes, and they still had his scent on them. Jarrad made his way around the room, reminiscing about everything He saw or touched, and there on his dresser was a note with his name on it. With all the turmoil, he never noticed it sitting there before. Jarrad tore it open and read.

My Dearest Beloved Jarrad,

I woke up this morning thinking about you. As I lay there in bed thinking about you, I realized there was something very wrong. I know I should have called someone right away. I can hear you fuming, but I had to tell you about how much you mean to me and that I am not abandoning you like so many before me have. Jarrad, you're my love, my life, my best friend, and my soul mate. I love you so much. Just remember that in the days that come.

Now, you have to promise me something important. Go find that Amish man who tore your world apart; talk with him, yell at him, or do what it takes to release that pain you have harbored in your heart. Set yourself free of that pain, and maybe, just maybe, you'll find out that he had no choice in the matter. Jarrad, Jeremiah Berkholter lives in Wasksa, PA. Promise one day soon you will go.

43

I better go now; remember, I love you without conditions. Be happy! You are so loved.

Your loving husband,

Jon

Jarrad felt his gentle, loving touch for just a second, and then he sobbed and sobbed until there were no more tears to come. He went downstairs and joined his family and friends. He saw this very sweet-looking, tiny little woman sitting by herself, trying so hard to keep it together and not succeeding. "Hi, I am Jarrad, Jon's husband, and you are?"

"Meredith Harper, Jon was my boss for nearly twenty years."

"Oh, yes, I remember you. Jon told me you were the most wonderful secretary in the world. We've met several times before, and under much better circumstances, Jon adored you."

She flung herself into his arms. "Not as much as he adored you," she whispered.

Jarrad just felt that they would be friends from that moment on, and they were.

The days passed, and the children went back to their lives. He missed them the second the door closed, but he knew that life had to go on, and so it did.

The kids were gone, working, starting families of their own, and just living life to its fullest.

Jarrad found himself working hard, spending time with friends, and traveling. Meredith became his closest friend, and now his constant traveling companion. They were perfect together, loved all the same things, and became inseparable. They went to Europe on their first vacation together. Jarrad spent more money on things for the kids than he did on the entire cost of the trip. He also had a picture of Jon painted by an artist in Paris from a snapshot he carried in his wallet. It was hung in the living room.

The kids settled in Boston and Philadelphia, and two of his five brothers had moved to the east coast with the other two working on getting there, so Jarrad decided there was no reason for him to stay so far away. Samuel and his bride, Connie, were expecting their first baby. He was not going to miss out on seeing his grandchildren any time he wanted to, rather than only once or twice a year. Anna Marie announced her engagement to the guy she'd been dating and was now planning a spring wedding. He wasn't missing out on that, either. Jarrad found a great position in Lancaster, PA.

Meredith understood his reasons for leaving but burst into tears every time he mentioned it. They were having lunch one day, and he asked her, "Mer, what keeps you here?"

She stopped and stared at him for a second. "Really? Nothing. I've no family except you and the kids. I have a job I like, but with Jon gone, it isn't much fun. Why?" she asked quietly.

"Honey, you need to job search, find a job, and move with me to Pennsylvania!"

"I couldn't. I haven't even thought about moving, but I could at least look, right?" Jarrad heard the excitement rise in her voice. That spark she had was twinkling brightly in her eyes.

Two days later, she called and told Jarrad she found a terrific job and would be interviewing for it tomorrow. She flew east and never made it back.

Jarrad packed up her apartment and had the stuff shipped to her.

He sold the home he'd shared with Jon. It truly was difficult to let it go, but an adorable gay couple fell in love with it and bought it. Jon would be so proud that he'd held out for the best price and the best people. Jarrad moved on very quietly with his life. He stopped at the grave site to talk with Jon before he took off for his new home five hundred miles away.

Jon wasn't there. He could feel it. Jarrad knew that he was busy doing what he did best, watching over their children and him. At that moment, he knew he wasn't leaving him behind but taking him with him.

Over the next few years, the women in his life, Anna Marie and Meredith, aka Mer, tried to fix him up with men they thought were *just perfect* for him, but either they weren't interested, interesting, or he wasn't interested. They finally started backing off. Jarrad guessed they both thought he was hopeless.

Baby Jonathan Samuel Stewart Upton was born and grew like a weed. Bop-Bop was his first word, and it thrilled Jarrad that the baby called him that. The little shit just won his heart.

Anna Marie's wedding was just beautiful. She put on a production, but it was still all centered around their wedding vows. A couple of things really touched Jarrad's heart. She had him walk her down the aisle, and the other was she had a special place reserved for her dad. Jarrad could feel Jon there the whole day. It truly was a spectacular day.

Connie and Samuel surprised Jarrad on his forty-sixth birthday with the announcement of a second baby coming. He was over the moon. Two days after Connie's announcement, Anna Marie made her own announcement, "Pop, I have some very important news for you. Mikkel and I are expecting." Jarrad jumped around, acting the fool. "Pop, Pop, listen, this is important!" she scolded.

He froze. "Is there something wrong? Are you okay, baby girl?" He went into panic mode.

"Pop, once again, you didn't let me finish. Pop, we're having triplets!"

He stood there looking dumbfounded. "Are you sure? Stupid question, I know, but I'm in shock."

"Pop, breathe a second. We're going to need everyone's help. Connie and Samuel will have their hands full, and with our babies coming within a month of each other, life around our family will be hectic." Boy, she wasn't kidding.

Samuel and Connie's baby boy, Jarrad Carlson Thomas Stewart Upton, came right on time. He was perfect and beautiful, just like his parents.

His Anna Marie was having a time of it. She was enormous and uncomfortable. Those little babies held on for dear life, and she carried them to 38 weeks. The most amazing part was that she delivered them naturally. She had a team of doctors willing to let her try, and his baby girl came through it like a trouper. Three perfect baby girls were identical. Sally Rose came first, then Michelle Rose, and finally Joanna Rose. They were the most beautiful baby girls in the world. Both Mer and Jarrad took turns going to Mikkel and Anna Marie's to help out, but it just wasn't enough. Jarrad knew that the young couple was just barely keeping it together. He decided to get them a live-in nanny. Anna Marie sobbed, and Mikkel hugged his neck. Sheila McKenzie was a godsend for them all. Anna Marie told him he saved her life and marriage. Always the drama queen, that one. Mikkel adores her. You can tell by the way he looks at her.

Chapter Seven: Jeremiah and Jarrad—Life Is Strange

In the spring that he turned forty-eight, Mer and Jarrad went on the two-week road trip they'd been talking about for years. Traveling through Amish country. Okay, deep down, Jarrad hoped to maybe at least see Jeremiah, because he'd never gotten up the nerve to go looking for him. He'd probably not recognize him now anyway, nor Jeremiah him.

What a wonderful time Mer and Jarrad had. They laughed and talked and shopped. "I bet I bought five grand's worth of Amish stuff, quilts, some furniture, hand-carved animal figures, a bunch of other stuff, and a truckload of stuff for the kids," he told Mer.

Into the second week of their shopping spree, they entered a shop in a village they visited for the first time. An adorable little Amish girl bounced over to them, greeting them, only to stop in her tracks, turn tail, and run screaming away. "Papa! Papa! I found him. He's in our store! Papa, come quick!"

"What did you do?" Mer accused Jarrad.

"What? I was standing here right beside you," Jarrad snapped back.

Mer wandered off in her need to outdo him with finding the most unusual thing. Jarrad found a quilt that he just had to have and then started looking at the beautiful wood carvings.

"Jarrad, you need to see this!" Meredith nearly screamed at him.

He started meandering in her direction, and when he turned to see what she squawked about, he saw five beautifully painted portraits. "They are all of me!" He just stood there gaping at them. "How on earth? This can't be me. It must be just a coincidence," he managed to barely say out loud.

"I'm very sorry, but these aren't for sale, not now or ever." a deep voice with a not-so-thick German accent said. It was so damn familiar. Tears welled up in Jarrad's eyes. He knew that second that it was Jeremiah.

Meredith looked at him so strangely, and then awareness came over her face. "Excuse me, I saw some quilts over there." She pointed and left. She was incredibly obvious.

Jarrad slowly turned to where the voice came from. There was the little girl about to burst as she bounced up and down. His eyes left her, rising up to look the man in the eyes that stood beside her. Jarrad knew the second their gazes met he knew him.

"Awk, no, Goot God, Jarrad." Suddenly two strong arms engulfed him. Jeremiah was a stranger, but yet so familiar. He smelled the same. Jarrad's heart pounded in his ears.

As he gained his wits, he pushed him back. "Jeremiah." His voice came across as distant and cold, and he knew it instantly.

"Oh my, Jarrad, I knew you were mad, but I never thought you could hate me." He heard Jeremiah's sadness. Jarrad looked toward his daughter and then back at him. He clearly understood. "Lydia Anne, go find your big sister and stay with her. Papa has business here, not for little ears."

"Okay, Papa." She bubbled and skipped away, shouting to whoever would listen, "I found him. I found him."

He turned to Jarrad. "You never wrote to me, Jarrad. Why?"

Jarrad felt that hurt and anger he'd buried so long ago

come rushing to life like an erupting volcano. "Where was I to send it? Can you answer that? Or maybe you just expected me to put it in a bottle and throw it to the wind? Tell me, Jeremiah, with no idea of where you were, how was I supposed to write you?" His voice was low, but the anger spewed out of him.

"Jarrad, I left you a letter, telling you of my love and why I had to go immediately and how you could get to me. I swear this. Perhaps Sally and Fred thought better of it and destroyed it?" Jeremiah almost pleaded with him.

"You got to be kidding me. They were nearly as heartbroken as I was, and after I nearly killed—never mind, they would have never done that, not ever!" Now Jarrad's voice started to get louder, loud enough to attract Mer's attention. "All you left of yourself was an Amish shirt with a note pinned to it about *your best friend*." Jarrad got more upset and angrier by the second.

"That shirt was to be for our wedding day." His voice was tender but had much pain in it.

An elderly man stepped out from somewhere in the back. "*Was geschieht hier*?" he asked in German.

"Father, stay away from this. Wait!"

The old man looked at Jarrad and then at the pictures, and then back at him. His eyes widened, and he turned to his son. "*Dies ist nicht gut*," he said quietly to his son.

"Father, so you know who this is then, correct?"

"Ya, it be best dat he goes from here," the old man said to them both.

"Father, those many years back when you came to get me because Momma was dying."

"VE will not speak of this." The old man turned to walk away.

"Vater, you are no longer head of this household. That would be me. You will stay."

The elderly Amish man stopped and turned toward his son.

"Father, we will speak English now so that Jarrad understands. Father, did you take the letter I wrote to Jarrad?"

"Vat difference does it make now? Dat time is gone now." Jeremiah's father was firm but polite.

"Answer me!" Jeremiah nearly shouted as he spat out the words. It took the old man aback. Jarrad was pretty shocked, too, as he never remembered him ever raising his voice.

"I did, I vanted this whole mess over, and it happened just as I knew it vould."

"No, Papa, it did not. I believed that Jarrad had moved on without me as he never wrote to me telling me he would come. So, after six years of waiting, I married Lydia out of loneliness, and she was my best friend. She knew that Jarrad was my only one true love and that I was heartbroken, but there would be no other than Jarrad. Yes, Papa, I loved her but as a friend and companion but not as a woman should have been loved."

"Awk, dat iz a lie. You had kinder, five of them, as a matter of fact." The smug look he gave Jarrad hurt, and Jeremiah saw it.

"*Es gibt mehr als einen Weg, um einen Hirsch,* Papa *Haut.* Oops, sorry, Jarrad, there is more than one way to skin a deer." His father turned red as a beet, not sure if it was from anger or embarrassment. "I love each of my children with all my heart. I was not baptized, and you know it, and you always knew why, didn't you? We moved to this progressive Amish settlement because they understand the heart and soul of people and look for the good in all as a true Amish man should. Lydia loved it here, as do my children and I. I never asked you to come, but wanted you to stay so you would not be alone in this world. Father, so, this is Jarrad Stewart, the man you caused much pain and suffering. That is not the

Amish way, is it?"

The old man turned and walked away. Jeremiah stood looking shocked at his father's response, but the elderly Amish man returned almost immediately. He walked up to Jarrad and stuck out a very old, yellowed envelope. "Dis belongs to you. I'm sorry I was the cause of your pain and suffering." He nodded his head and left.

Jarrad realized that after all these years, Jeremiah had not abandoned him at all. He was just lost to him due to deception. Slowly, he turned the unopened letter over, and there was his name written on it.

"You must open it and read this letter so you know how I felt then and have always felt for you."

Jarrad's hands shook, and he felt a little sick to his stomach. He handed him back the letter. "Not now, Jeremiah, not after all I went through. That part of my life is dead. It died in the hospital twenty-eight years ago when my life turned to nothing because you were gone."

"Like hell it is!" Meredith came out of nowhere and slapped the back of Jarrad's head. She was fuming mad. "You *are* going to read that God damned letter, and you're going to tell this man about your life, and you're going to listen to him about his life, or I will beat the living shit out of you right here and now."

Jarrad gaped, bug-eyed like a fish out of water. He'd never heard Meredith talk like that.

"Close your mouth and open that damn letter and read it. Now!"

He opened it and started reading, afraid not to.

My Dearest Jarrad,

I'm not much of a letter writer, but I will try to tell you it all in this letter. There is no time for me to tell you all I feel in person, so I must try to do it here.

Mama is dying, and there is only a short time left. I must go to her and help with the family. My Rumspringa is over, and I must become a man today and take up my responsibilities within my family. That means I have to go back to Commera, this is a small Amish village outside of Wilton. Wilton is on the map. I hope you understand that as an Amish man, I must fulfill my promise to come back and decide all further happenings in my life from my home.

Now I will tell you about how important you are in my life. When all is finished with your schooling, come to me, and we will make a life together. I love you, Jarrad Stewart, with all my heart. I will never love another. So please write to me and tell me when you are coming to me. There are no phones at all in my small village, and it is fifteen miles to the nearest one. Once I hear from you, I will call, that I promise. Life will be hard for us, but no matter what, I know our love will get us through, even if we have to move to another Amish community. I'm sorry to tell you this now, but I can live no other way but Amish. I tried so hard to live as you do, but it is not me. I did try and tell you so many times, but the words got stuck in my gullet, and I could not say them for fear you would not love me anymore. I pray with all my soul that you will be able to come and be Amish with me. You can write to me:

Jeremiah Berkholter, C/O Berkholter Farm, Commera, OH. It will get to me, I promise.

Please, my dear beloved Jarrad, do not be mad with me. I have to go. Please come to me soon.

Yours Forever,

Jeremiah Berkholter.

Ps. If I do not hear from you, I will understand that you do not love me. It will break my heart, but I will not bother you ever again.

Jarrad kept looking at the letter, and he read it over one more time. He didn't look at Jeremiah. But when Meredith elbowed him, he looked up. There stood Jeremiah, looking at him with tear-filled eyes. His heart could no longer stand it, and his soul wanted to be with his soul mate. He flung his arms around Jeremiah's neck, and their lips met. He held Jarrad so tightly that he could scarcely breathe. Jarrad needed his strength and to feel him close.

"Großer Gott im Himmel!" He heard Jeremiah's father.

"Eww! Kissing!" some little child squeaked out.

"Stop that immediately. You two need to get a room," Meredith said, laughing.

But it was the voice of a young man that brought this to a halt. "Papa, what are you thinking? PDA right here in our store? You couldn't wait until we got home for this?" The young man sounded so grown up and mature.

Jeremiah released him, and Jarrad turned and saw five children staring at them. Jarrad felt surprised that not one of them seemed shocked or upset in the least at their father kissing a man. What the hell?

"Come meet my big brood. The tall, good-looking man in the back is the eldest, Jarrad. He's turning sixteen this month. He's the one that keeps order in my household." Jarrad let out a surprised gasp. Jeremiah just smiled. "Yah, he's named for you. That beauty next to him is Sally Rose. She's a very wise thirteen-year-old. She keeps the children in line and safe."

Again, Jarrad was caught off guard. He felt the tears rolling out of his eyes.

Jeremiah continued. "This fine young upstart is Fredrick. He's my ten-year-old farmer and a true Amish man, and next to him is Isaac, who's nine going on fifty. He's going to be a doctor, a lawyer, and a teacher. And this little monkey is Minnie Mouse."

"Hey!" she spouted in horror.

"Sorry, this is our precious Lydia Anne, who's turning four tomorrow."

"Papa, I'm going to be five tomorrow!" She acted totally indignant.

"Father you have met, and their mother went to be with God almost five years ago."

He looked at little Lydia Anne with such love. Somehow Jarrad understood his wife had died during childbirth.

"I'm pleased to meet you all. What a beautiful family you all are."

"*Ach*, that they are fine-looking is not important. It's only important that they work hard and love Gott." The old man huffed off, not really angry or upset, just expressing his Amish outlook on life. Then, from the back room, he shouted, "Courting first, then kissing."

Jeremiah's eyes nearly bugged out, and he turned beet red.

It was Meredith bursting into uncontrolled laughter that got everyone started.

It was at this time that Jarrad, Jeremiah's oldest son, recognized him as the man in the pictures. He looked at Jarrad, then the pictures, and then back again. Suddenly this big boy hugged Jarrad and hugged him hard. Jarrad could feel that the boy was crying. He suddenly stepped back. "That was for Mama. I promised her before she died that if Papa ever found you, I would give you a big hug and welcome you to our family. Mama tried so hard to find you for Papa that she even went to the library and searched for you on the internet, which, of course, is against the Amish rules, but Mama was not really big on following the rules. She never could find you. Sorry, Papa, I promised Mama not to tell you until he came to you, and now he's here." Jeremiah's son looked overly emotional and tried so hard to get himself back into control. Jarrad did what he would have with his own son and pulled him back in for another hug. He stayed until he was back in control like an Amish man should be, and then stepped back.

Jarrad stood there looking at Jeremiah and his family and realized that he probably would never be part of it. "Mer, we need to get going."

She stood there gaping at him like he was some freak or something, and then with lightning reflexes, she nearly bitch slapped him to the floor, and that had hurt.

"*Ach!* Woman, we do not do such things here. Violence is not our way." Jeremiah stepped in front of Jarrad while he was gaining his composure and rubbing his cheek.

"Get out of my way, Amish Man, or you'll be next." She moved him to the side and was up in Jarrad's face. "Listen to me, you little twirp, and you listen good. For twenty-eight years, you have had an ache in your heart that could not and would not go away. You believed that this goober here just up and left you, abandoned you. Why he didn't come back and get you is a whole other story." Meredith whipped a *speak, and I will personally neuter you* look on them both. "Don't you dare even breathe loud while I'm talking. You two have a chance at something special, and I have a chance at getting a really big discount on Amish furniture, quilts, and the like, so the two of you will be staying here and talking this thing out, or I will take you both out to the woodshed and beat the living shit out of you both, and I can do it, too! I'm taking Grandpa and the kids for ice cream down the street, so you two work it out, or I'll work you over. Old man, get your ugly black hat, and let's go. Hey, Miss Lydia Anne, what's your favorite flavor of ice cream?" It was like an old-time movie. Everyone got in line and followed her out.

Young Jarrad asked Meredith on the way out, "Can you teach me how to do that?"

"Do what?" She was confused. "Make Papa and Jarrad shut up and listen." He was dead serious.

Mr. Berkholter piped in, "Wouldn't mind learnin' dat, too."

"First of all, you have to be a woman." Meredith knew her stuff.

"Forget it!" they both said.

Everyone was laughing as they left Jeremiah's shop.

Jarrad and Jeremiah stood staring at each other. It was an

awkward moment for both of them. Each needed to say something to the other, but neither thought they should go first. Jarrad felt a terrible instinct to turn and bolt out the door, but Jeremiah must have sensed it and sidestepped, so he blocked his exit route.

Suddenly, it all burst out of Jarrad. "Jeremiah, why didn't you come back to see why I didn't come to you? Why?" The tears welled up in his eyes, and nothing could stop them.

"Oh, Jarrad, if I'd known you never got the letter I wrote, nothing would have stopped me from coming to you, but I believed your silence was the answer to my letter. Jarrad Stewart, I never for one second stopped loving you. I love and loved others, but only you have that place in my heart that makes me complete."

"I felt so alone. Life was not worth living without you, Jeremiah. It took me years just to want to live again. When Sally and Fred found me that morning after you left, I was almost dead, and they —"

"Stop! My God, no, I could have lost you forever? Oh God, thank you for Sally and Fred." He pulled him into his strong embrace and held him close. Jarrad felt his body shaking, and then he realized Jeremiah was crying.

Ding-a-ling. The shop bell alerted them that someone had entered the shop. He tried to back away, but Jeremiah was having none of that. "We are closed for the afternoon." He stated flatly. The shop bell stopped ringing, so that person must have exited. That was when he kissed Jarrad so passionately that he just dissolved into his arms. He stepped back, reached inside his clothing, and pulled out a gold chain. He saw them, the half-heart that matched the one Jarrad was wearing. The one Jeremiah had given him so many Christmases ago and beside it, the two gold wedding bands that he'd given Jeremiah that same Christmas. Jarrad knew at that moment that it was either going to be the two of them forever or it was going to be the last time he would ever see Jeremiah again.

Jeremiah decided the answer to that and gently pulled Jarrad close, took his hand, and walked to the front door of the store. Jarrad thought it was time for him to go anyway. Sadness filled his heart as he followed him. Again, to be pushed aside, but this time, Jarrad knew that Jeremiah had his family, and they had to come first.

Tearing up, he needed to get out of there so his grief wouldn't be seen. But when they reached the door, Jeremiah stretched out his hand and locked it. He must have seen the emotion and sadness Jarrad felt because, within seconds, he swooped Jarrad up and carried him to the back of the store.

"What? You don't think for one second you're leaving me after it took forever for me to find you? Do you?"

Jarrad shook his head and snuggled in close to him, inhaling his wonderful scent.

Jeremiah smiled at Jarrad. "I'm quite sure I remember just where we left off the last time we made love." He did that eyebrow thing, and Jarrad saw the passion in Jeremiah's eyes. Still as strong as a bull, Jeremiah carried Jarrad with little or no effort to the back of the store. He kicked open a back room, and there was a bed there. "Napping place for the little ones," he said, as if he could read Jarrad's questioning mind.

Jeremiah's ability to make Jarrad's body respond in every way had not changed at all. It was like they were never apart for all those many years. He knew just how to make Jarrad's body respond to his. Jeremiah's lips knew Jarrad's lips. Jeremiah's huge cock pressed hard and throbbed against Jarrad's. The passion swelled, and they were about to explode.

"Jarrad, have you been with others?" he whispered. It all stopped.

Jarrad felt Jon was being forgotten. "Yes. I was very much in love with the Daddy to my children. We were together for more than twenty years. I just lost that wonderful man not so long ago."

"Did you love him more than me?" Jeremiah asked him.

"I'm not sure that I could have ever loved anyone the way I've been in love with you. Jon knew that, but he loved me unconditionally. He was a very good and caring man."

Jeremiah took a deep breath and said, "I'm so glad you had someone. I had Lydia, not like you had Jon, but it was very similar. The thought of you being alone hurt my heart. Lydia always knew when I was thinking about you. I have to admit I lost part of my soul for a while, but now it's back. Jarrad, so you know, there will be no other men in your life from now on." Jeremiah suddenly started acting very Amish. "The past is gone. I may be a liberal Amish man, but Amish I am, and I hope we'll make a wonderful life together." Having said that, he returned to the passionate man he was just before the conversation started.

"Ah, Jeremiah, don't I have any say in this?" Jarrad groused to him.

"No." That was all Jeremiah said, and his mouth met Jarrad's, and the love they'd missed was on its way back. "Too much clothes," he said. He started to undress Jarrad. His expensive Armani shirt was buttonless in seconds, and before he could protest, they were both naked. It was like no time had passed between them. Jarrad could feel his hard cock press against him, his still very muscular body maneuvering Jarrad's so they were in the right position. Still, ever the stallion and dominant male, Jeremiah knew what he wanted and how to get there. It was only about a half hour of lovemaking, but it was beyond wonderful.

Jeremiah sat up and took off his gold necklace. Jarrad's smile turned to a pained expression.

Jeremiah saw the look, and his expression deepened. "What's wrong?" He took the two rings and placed them in

Jarrad's hand. "Why are you looking so hurt and sad? Don't you want to marry me?"

Jarrad swallowed hard. "Are you asking me to really marry you?"

Jeremiah leaned back a little to look into Jarrad's eyes. "I promised you, my love, long ago. I wore those rings around my neck in hopes of marrying you. So, are you going to marry this old man?"

Jarrad wrapped his arm around Jeremiah's neck and sobbed. After a few moments, he shook his head. "I want that more than anything."

As they lay there absorbing the passion from each other, they heard, "Papa, where are you? Meredith says I should bother you. Why?"

Jeremiah shouted out, "Lydia Rose, you stay there. I'll come to you."

Little Lydia Rose put a quick stop to their afterglow as they scrambled to clean up and find their clothes. How would Jarrad explain his shirt? Jarrad picked it up and showed it to his lover. Jeremiah burst into laughter. It was the warm and contagious laughter Jarrad so clearly remembered.

"Aw, fuck it, and I'll just tuck it in and hope no one says a word. I clearly must be dreaming. Mer will absolutely not miss this."

They dressed just in time, and the back door flew open. "What the hell did you do to your shirt?" Meredith stupidly asked. "Oh, God, never mind." Now everyone noticed.

"Vhat? Are you both animals?" Jeremiah's father spouted off.

"No, Papa, but we are definitely human." Jeremiah was looking at Jarrad with such love that he no longer cared about his shirt.

It was then they heard the teenager's moans of embarrassment. Jeremiah's oldest two were about to die of embarrassment. They stood there with red faces and looked everywhere but at Jarrad and Jeremiah.

"Papa, you smell funny," Lydia Rose so innocently commented.

That was it for Meredith and Grandpa Berkholter. They both crumbled into uncontrollable laughter. Soon, everyone laughed, even the little guys who had no idea why, but they laughed.

Jarrad started to go out the door. "Jarrad, where are you going?" He heard the panic in Jeremiah's voice.

"To my car to get clean clothes and some wipes to clean up." He reached up and gently touched Jeremiah's face. "I'll be back in just a few minutes."

"I'll go with you," Jeremiah said. There was almost a *please* in his voice.

"Sure, but the car is just across the street." He took Jeremiah's hand.

"Papa, remember yourself, no PDA," young Jarrad scolded. He was so like his father in looks and mannerisms, Jarrad just had to smile.

Jeremiah smiled. "Ya, just like his old Papa."

The memory of that day way back when flooded back into Jarrad's mind, and tears started to roll.

"Papa, what have you done?" Little Lydia Rose scolded.

Jarrad smiled and said, "Precious baby, these are tears of a wonderful memory that brought joy back into my heart, and one day I'll tell you about them." He reached down and kissed her head, and she latched onto his neck, needing a reassuring hug.

Jarrad and Jeremiah left and returned, and they looked refreshed and less crumpled.

Within the hour, Meredith and Jarrad followed his new

family to what would become his new home. He looked at his beloved friend and said, "I'm not sure what I was expecting when we started this journey. I guess I hoped to find Jeremiah but never believed I would. I wasn't expecting to find my long-lost love, and then to find our love is as strong as ever."

CHAPTER EIGHT: THE LIFE OF DREAMS

Several weeks had passed since Jarrad stepped into Jeremiah's shop. Many things had changed for his family. Not only had it gotten bigger, but life with Jeremiah couldn't be more wonderful. Not to say that the transition was an easy one.

Jarrad smiled and said to Jeremiah, "I was just thinking about our wedding."

He invited his entire family. Jeremiah had told Jarrad back then, "We will have a family wedding. Not too big, not too small."

Jarrad looked at him with raised eyebrows and dark threatening eyes.

"That would be okay with you?" Jeremiah sheepishly asked him.

Jarrad couldn't help but laugh. "Yes, but we'll have to make sure we invite some friends, too. Like Meredith and her boyfriend."

Jeremiah looked at him perplexed. "She's family."

Jarrad and Jeremiah planned a simple but beautiful wedding. All of their children and grandchildren were there celebrating with them. Much to Jarrad's surprise, many of the surrounding neighbors also attended the ceremony.

Papa Berkholter announced, "Love is gute. It's the Amish way."

Their small wedding, it seemed, turned out to be quite large. It didn't matter. Everyone who attended brought food, so there was plenty to go around.

The Justice of the Peace called the wedding to order. He performed an Amish-type wedding.

"Are you, Jeremiah and Jarrad, here of your own free will and without hesitation?"

"We are," the two men answered.

"Are you of like mind to be joined in marriage?"

Jarrad and Jeremiah answered, "We are."

"Are you here to promise your love and devotion to each other?"

"We are."

"They have promised themselves to each other. May their marriage be long and filled with love. You are married."

Jeremiah pulled Jarrad to him and kissed him. The guests applauded, and the feast began.

"Papa and Papa Two, you were yucky and kissed in front of everyone," Lydia Rose scolded, shaking her finger at them.

"Your Papa just got carried away," Jarrad teased.

The newlyweds mingled and chatted with the guests. Grandpa Berkholter talked and laughed loudly. Jarrad commented to Jeremiah, "This is out of character for him. He's usually so reserved."

He and Jeremiah walked over to where Grandpa stood. Jeremiah got close and suddenly stopped. He stepped a little closer and sniffed. "Papa, you've been in the hard cider."

Grandpa Berkholter looked like a deer caught in the headlights. "No, I don't think so," he said and started giggling like a little kid.

"Jarrad and Fredrick, please take Papa and have him lie down."

With one on each side, they started gently moving their grandfather. They both sniffed him and then, wide-eyed, they looked at their father. Jeremiah rolled his eyes and nodded, affirming their suspicions. Off they went, with Grandpa giggling all the way.

Jarrad laughed. "He's going to feel like shit tomorrow."
Shaking his head, Jeremiah said, "No doubt about it."

When Jarrad's two children, all of his brothers and their
spouses and children had first arrived, they'd totally freaked
out. The whole Amish thing threw them for a loop for the first
few days. Anna Marie and Samuel came around when they
saw the love that flowed between Jarrad and Jeremiah. Jeremiah's loving spirit, and wonderful, accepting attitude made
his children and all the families fall in love with him, too. It
helped that Meredith's bulldog personality appeared and
threatened them all.

Jarrad's grandkids loved the farm, the shop, and the small
town. Anna Marie dressed the triplets in little girl Amish
clothes, and she brought them to the shop to surprise Jeremiah. He and his father stood staring for a moment, then Jeremiah knelt down, spread his arms wide, and said, "Come to
your grandpa and give him a big hug." The little girls flew
into his arms. Jeremiah loved being their grandpa, and even
the old man couldn't help loving all his new great-grandchil-
dren. They love their Grandpapa, too.

Jarrad and Jeremiah's families grew and grew. Thank God
the farmhouse was huge, with nine bedrooms and four baths.
The company came and went constantly.

Jarrad opened a midwife birthing center in the small city
close to them. He hired a staff of ten, and they were constantly
busy. Grandpapa Berkholter scoffed at Jarrad when he
opened his center. "Vhat kind of vomen allows such tings?
You waste gute money." Now, he shook his head and avoided
the conversation entirely. Jarrad needed to be coaxed by Jeremiah to hire help so they wouldn't be apart so much.

Ultimately, Jarrad only worked two or three days a week
at the center. The rest of the time, he and Jeremiah were doing
things together. Sometimes they were being what Lydia Rose

called *yucky*.

The paintings of Jarrad, the ones found by Meredith in Jeremiah's shop, now hung on their bedroom walls. *Pictures of Hope,* as Jeremiah called them. Their life was perfect. The emptiness had disappeared.

One evening, after a very large family get-together had ended, Jeremiah turned to Jarrad. "We need to go." Jeremiah pulled Jarrad in close. "I mean right now. I need you."

Jarrad smiled and said, "Even after all these years, you still lust after me?"

"Until the day I die. We really need to go to our room."

That ended the conversation. Jeremiah took Jarrad's hand and pulled him into the house and up into their bedroom. He closed the door and locked it.

"Fate brought us together twice. I'll never stop needing you. That's Amish love."

ABOUT THE AUTHOR

I'm a retired educator. I live on a farm in the northeast Georgia Mountains, where we raise miniature horses. I spend time writing and tending the many animals on the farm. I live with my teenage son and my elderly father. Both are my inspiration.

www.ingramcontent.com/pod-product-compliance
Lightning Source LLC
Chambersburg PA
CBHW071126130626
46555CB00010B/1585